The Diary

of

Robin's Toys

Ken and Angie Lake

Leon the Lion

Published by Sweet Cherry Publishing Limited
53 St. Stephens Road,
Leicester, LE2 1GH
United Kingdom

First Published in the UK in 2013

ISBN: 978-1-78226-028-8

Title: Leon the Lion - The Diaries of Robin's Toys

Printed and Bound By Nutech Print Services, India

Every Toy Has a Story to Tell

Have you ever seen an old toy, perhaps in a cupboard, or in the attic or loft? Have you ever seen how sad they look at car boot sales, unwanted and unloved? Well, look at them closely, because every toy has a story to tell, and the older, the more decrepit, the more scruffy, the more tatty the toy is, the more interesting its story could be. Here are just a few of those toys and their stories.

16th September, 09.25

It was Sunday morning, and Robin opened the curtains to a shiny world. The whole street was glossy; it had been raining earlier that morning, but it had just stopped.

Robin was lost in his thoughts. He couldn't help thinking about how his team had lost the football match, and it was all because of one little boy, John Paul Jones; or JP for short.

He had joined the Busy Bees football team a few weeks ago, and yesterday he had played his first match as goalkeeper. But it had been a total disaster. The Busy Bees had lost 5-1, the opposite team having walked all over them. This had never happened before.

Robin had overheard JP's mum talking to the coach, Dickinson, a few weeks earlier.

"I know JP isn't the best footballer, but he needs to start meeting other children.

"He seems happy to spend all his time playing in the garden, birdwatching, growing plants from seeds ... he just loves nature!

"But I've told him he's never going to make friends by staying at home and playing in the garden on his own. At least if he plays football he's out in the open air getting some exercise, and maybe he'll make some friends."

Robin could see that Mrs Jones had good intentions, but this was definitely not the solution. After yesterday's match, none of the other children even wanted to speak to JP.

Robin had felt really sorry for him, so he went up to him and said, "Don't worry, we all have good times and bad times. I'm having a birthday party. Would you like to come?"

Suddenly, the bright red sun peeped out from behind a heavy grey cloud.

"Wow, look, Mum! There's a beautiful rainbow."

Its arc stretched from one end of the street right into the distance.

As Robin stared at the rainbow, he thought of the rhyme he had learned in school to remember the order of the colours.

Start at the outside, then say: Richard of York gave battle in vain. Then take the first letter of each word: Richard, first letter R for Red. Then Of, first letter O for Orange; York, Y for Yellow; Gave, G for Green; Battle, B for Blue; In, I for Indigo; Vain, V for Violet.

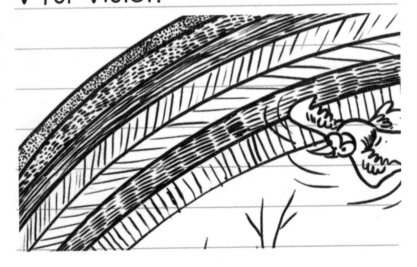

He looked at the rainbow
again and checked the colours.
Yes, it worked!

He looked back at the
street and remembered that he
had a birthday coming up, and
dreamed of having a party
with all of his friends.

Then Robin's thoughts were interrupted.

Beep, beep! Beep, beep!

It was Grandad's little red car.

"Come on, Robin, it's time to go to the car boot sale."

"Oh, Grandad, have you seen that beautiful rainbow? Can we follow it and find out where it ends?"

"Yes, come on then. Do you know what they say about the end of the rainbow?"

"No, not really, Grandad. What do they say?"

"They say that at the end of the rainbow you will find a pot of gold."

"Oh, Grandad, let's follow it then!"

So that's what they did, and what do you think was at the end of the rainbow? Yes, you're right... It was the car boot sale.

"Okay, Grandad, where is the pot of gold?"

"Well, Robin, I think this may be as close as you can get to it."

He handed Robin 50 pence to spend on a toy.

Then they wandered around the stalls looking for an interesting toy to buy.

"Oh, I know," said Robin, "let's have a look on Beryl's Bargains and see what she has this week."

She had a lot of old DVDs, you know, the sort that are given away with the Sunday newspaper. There were also a few old clocks; her husband had collected them once upon a time!

Once upon a time he collected clocks ... That sounds like a bit of a story to me!

Robin didn't see anything which interested him, so he said, "Excuse me, Mrs Bargains, do you have any interesting toys this week?"

"Interesting toys?" she mumbled, scratching her head. "Ah yes, what about this toy lion?" She held it up and waved it around.

"Oh, may my grandad have a look at it, please?"

"Yes, of course he can."

Grandad looked the lion straight in the eyes and went into one of his trances. He had a word with the lion, and then winked at Robin.

"Yes, Robin, he has an interesting story to tell. Ask her how much she wants for him."

"Alright. Mrs Bargains, how much is the lion?"

"Oh yes, Leon the Lion."

She scratched her head again and thought for a while.

"You can have him for 75 pence."

"Oh, I'm sorry, I only have 50 pence to spend."

"Oh alright, go on then, just 50 pence for Leon the Lion. Shall I put him in a bag for you?"

"Alright, Robin, now that we have your toy, I need to get something for Grandma."

"What are you going to buy for her, Grandad?"

"Well, she needed a few bits and pieces for your... well, let's just say it's a surprise. Let's go to see Ian on Fraser's Foods."

"Oh, you mean Mr Broken-Biscuit."

"Good morning, Ian," said Grandad as they approached his stall.

"Good morning, Harry. What can I get for you today?"

"Mabel needs some tinned pineapple. Have you got any?"

"Have I got any? Harry, you would never believe it, but that new boy at my shop left the tap running and flooded the whole cellar. I had just bought a case of very expensive exotic tinned food and found it floating around with the other stuff.

"When I went down there, the water had soaked the labels and they had all come off. That boy will have to go!" and all the labels had come off. That boy will have to go!"

"So, Ian, how do you know what's inside the tins then?"

"Well, Harry, I have been in this business long enough to recognise the tins."

He rummaged around in his damaged case and handed

Grandad a big tin.

"Here we are, Harry, this looks like a tin of pineapple... this one is mangos in syrup, and this one here is peaches."

"That's amazing, Ian; you really know your stuff!"

"They may all look the same to the untrained eye, but a man with my level of expertise can spot a tin of pineapple at a hundred paces.

"And, as it's you and I have known you for such a long time, I will make you a special offer. You can have 5 different tins for the price of 6. Now, I can't say fairer than that! You won't get a deal like that anywhere else."

Grandad was wearing his confused face; he had never been very good at maths.

"Shall I put them in a bag for you?"

When they arrived back at Grandad's house, there were lots of wonderful smells, but before Robin could burst into the kitchen, Grandma rushed out into the hallway and closed the door behind her.

"Hmm, something smells REALLY good, Grandma!" said Robin.

"Well, I'm afraid that this week you'll have to wait until later to have your tea."

She turned to Grandad and whispered, "Harry, did you pick up the tinned fruit for the trifle?"

"Of course I did, dear," he answered, handing her the bag.

"Now, boys, why don't you go to the living room while I finish what I'm doing in the kitchen?"

41

Grandad and Robin made their way into the living room. Robin put the lion on the coffee table and Grandad cast his magic spell.

"Little toy, hear this rhyme,
Let it take you back in time,
Tales of sadness or of glory,
Little toy, reveal your story."

The lion twitched a bit and then thought about doing a little roar, but he knew deep down that he wasn't really the roaring kind.

So he shook his big bushy mane and swished his long tail.

"Hello, my name is Leon. Le...on the Li....on; it sort of rhymes a bit, doesn't it? I like rhymes. Anyway, who are you?"

"My name is Robin and this is my grandad."

"Hello, Robin; hello, Grandad. Where am I?"

"You are at home with us, sitting on our coffee table."

"Oh yes, so I am."

"We bought you from Beryl's Bargains at the car boot sale. We thought you looked interesting and would have a great story to tell us."

"How did you know that?"

"Well, Leon, my grandad has magical powers."

"*What sort of magical powers do you have, Grandad?*"

"I seem to have the ability to make toys talk."

"Oh, I see. Do you know anything about lions in general, where we come from and what we do all day long?"

"No, Leon, not very much. Why don't you tell us?"

"Alright. Are you both sitting comfortably?"

"Yes, thank you, Leon."

"Then I shall begin."

"Please do."

"Lions are big cats."

"Yes, Leon, we can see that."

"Don't interrupt, Robin, or I shall have to eat you."

"Eat me? Sorry, Leon."

"Only kidding! Right, as I was saying, lions are big cats, but not quite the biggest; that honour goes to the tiger. He's the one with stripes.

"In the wild we live in groups called prides, and I am proud of that. Proud of the pride! I made a funny joke; come on, Grandad, laugh! Oh alright, please yourself.

"A few of my wild cousins still live in Africa, and there are also some in Asia and a few in India. We tend to live on the plains, so I have no idea why lions are called Kings of the Jungle. Lions are known as carnivores; that means we eat meat."

"Does that include burgers?"

"No, sorry, Robin, they don't count. Anyway, we tend to hunt at night and sleep during the day when it's hot.

"Now, most people think that lions are fierce, ferocious,

scary and hairy. Well, not all of us are. I have never been into that strong-arm stuff; you know, all that strutting around, roaring and scaring people.

"I am a mild-mannered, timid sort of lion. I much prefer staying indoors, playing Snap and writing short stories and poetry."

"Writing short stories and poetry?"

"Yes, that's what I said. I hate being bossy and telling people what to do. But being the way I am has caused me lots of personal problems."

"What do you mean, Leon?"

"*Just listen and I will tell you. You see, I didn't have any proper friends, and no other lions wanted to be associated with me. Lions are quite particular about who they mix with. They are meant to be brave and butch, and they have an image to protect.*

"*I was bored with being alone and not having any mates. I wanted to meet people and be accepted for what I really was, a shy, gentle, poetry-writing lion.*

"One day I was at the supermarket having a moan to the girl on the checkout.

"I've got no friends, moan, moan, moan and more moaning.

" 'Why don't you get a job?'
she said. 'You'll meet lots of
people that way.'

"I hadn't even thought
about that before. So on the
way out I looked at the
noticeboard. There were
vacancies in the store, so I
went to the customer service
counter and picked up an
application form.

"I filled it in the way they had taught me at lion school and posted it back to the supermarket. About a week later, I was called in for an interview with the manager.

" 'We have a position coming up with our security staff,' he said.

" 'Oh no, I don't want that. I want to work on the check outs and meet lots and lots of nice people.'

" 'Don't be silly, Leon,' the manager said. 'You are a lion; you will scare the customers away.'

"I tried to explain about my gentle personality, but it was no good, the manager wouldn't change his mind. It would be security or nothing. So I decided to look for a job somewhere else.

"I wandered down the high street and looked in the window of a well-known employment agency.

"Wanted: Shop Sales Assistant. Yes, that is the ideal job for me, I thought. I would meet lots of people and make lots of friends. So I went in, filled in a form and waited for the manageress.

"She looked quite scared. 'You actually want to be in sales?' she gasped. 'I am sorry, that's just not possible. You are a lion; you will scare people and they will feel intimidated. Now, we may be able to find you a back room job, but definitely not a

customer service position.'
I was distraught they didn't
want me.

"The next advert I saw was a part-time job as a babysitter. Now, I had always liked children, so I applied. At the interview, I explained to the manager how gentle and kind I was, but he was not impressed.

" 'Yea okay, Leon, you may be the nicest lion in the pride, but what do you think would happen to my business if you got annoyed and started eating the kids? Sorry, man, I just can't risk it.'

"It was the same story with every job I applied for. I was beginning to get a bad reputation locally, and some adverts even stated: Lions need not apply."

"I was getting more and more depressed, so I went back to staying indoors and writing my poetry again.

"Several weeks later, I was sitting at home alone and listening to the radio; it was one of the local commercial stations. You know the type, 3 minutes of music and then 10 minutes of adverts.

"The announcer said, 'Would you like to work at our radio station? We currently have vacancies, no experience necessary. Just phone this number.' I had always fancied myself as a DJ, so I phoned them.

"I filled in the application form and went for the interview, but it was the same old story.

" 'Really sorry, Leon, your voice is much too deep and roary for radio.' My heart sank, and I got up to leave.

" 'Just a minute,' he said. 'It says on your form that your hobby is writing poetry. I am looking for someone to write the adverts and jingles. Are you interested in a trial?' "

"What's a jingle, Leon?"

"Oh, Robin, do I have to explain everything?"

"Yes, please."

"Well, a jingle is a little radio rhyme which is usually sung.

"Anyway, to get back to my story ... When I was offered the job, I said, 'Oh yes please! When can I start?'

" 'You can start now if you want to.'

"So that's what I did."

"Within a week, I had written lots and lots of things for the radio station. My adverts were so convincing that the companies sold lots more products, but my best work was always my jingles.

"This is one of mine; I wrote it for Lion Toothpaste. I am sure you must have heard it:

You should use LION TOOTHPASTE when you've been eating beef.

When you've used LION TOOTHPASTE you can really show your teeth.

You must use LION TOOTHPASTE, it really is the best.

*When you use LION
TOOTHPASTE you'll be a
roaring success.*

*"It's brilliant, isn't it? Would
you like to sing it with me?"*

"Err, not at the moment,
thank you, Leon."

"Anyway, they were so popular that the listening figures doubled, and the manager was so pleased that he offered me a permanent contract.

74

"Within a few months my work was known throughout the broadcasting industry. I had made lots of friends and was a very happy lion at last.

"In the radio business I soon became known as Le...on the Li...on, King of the Jingle."

"Thank you, Leon. That was a fascinating story."

And just as Leon finished his story, Grandma poked her head round the living room door.

"Hello, boys... Harry, I need to see you in the kitchen right away. It's private."

Grandad made his way into the kitchen and closed the door behind him. He was met by an angry Grandma, holding out a bag.

"Harry, I'm just making the trifle and I've realised that these tins don't have any labels on them. Which one is the pineapple?"

"Oh, that's easy, dear, it's this one," he said, pointing to the first one he saw.

He didn't want to look silly, so he just picked the top one. In any case it wouldn't make much difference: pineapple, peach, mango ... they could all be used in a trifle.

Grandma had already put in the sponge and the jelly.

"Alright, Harry, open the tin for me."

He was happy to help. Just as Grandma was about to pour

the pineapple into the jelly,
Grandad interrupted her.

"Quick, Mabel, look outside.
It's another rainbow!"

She looked out of the kitchen window.

"Oh yes, how pretty."

Grandad was very pleased with his quick save. Whether it was pineapple or peach, the contents of the tin were now in the jelly and no one would be any the wiser.

"I shall put this in the fridge to set for a bit before I put on the cream," Grandma said. "Keep Robin distracted while I load up the boot of the car with all these things I've made for his birthday party. We'll be off in half an hour."

Robin knew it was a special day, but he was still surprised to arrive home and be greeted by all his friends and family.

"Happy birthday!" they all shouted as he walked through the door. The house looked amazing! Mum and Dad had spent all morning decorating, and making sandwiches and party food.

Grandma had been busy
baking, and she'd brought pies,
cakes and the trifle.

All of Robin's friends were there, from school, football and the Scouts.

Even JP had turned up. Although he seemed to be mostly on his own, as the boys from football still weren't speaking to him.

"Here we are, boys!" said Grandma. "Gather round! Who wants trifle?"

Robin's friends gathered round the table and were each given a dish of Grandma's trifle. As they started spooning it into their mouths, there were some looks of confusion.

"Yuk! What's this?"

"Err, Grandma," said Robin, "is the trifle supposed to have tentacles?"

Grandma gave Grandad one of her scariest looks and he disappeared from the room.

"It's Aegina Gray," muttered JP, to everybody's bewilderment. "Aegina Gray – Marbled Octopus. It's a breed of octopus which comes from the Pacific Ocean. It's a great delicacy in Japan. You can even buy it in this country, in tins of course."

The room went silent.
Then Darren, one of the older
boy scouts, shouted, "COOL!"

Before you could say octopus trifle, Darren and a few of the other scouts had gone over to JP. They were poking and prodding at the trifle like they had just discovered an alien.

"So how do you know so much about this stuff, JP?" asked Darren.

"Oh, I find marine life really interesting; well, marine life, birds ... nature in general."

"Wow!" said Darren. "You should join the Scouts. We do loads of stuff out in nature. We have birdwatching badges ... and we even have a trip to the seaside coming up!"

"That sounds great!" said JP. "I didn't think I'd ever meet other people who like all those kinds of things."

Meanwhile, Grandma was having a few cross words with Grandad.

"Harry! Have you called
that Mr Fraser-Foods yet?"

"Oh yes, dear, don't worry, I called him as soon as I saw that look on your face."

"Well, what did he have to say for himself?"

"He said that tinned octopus is one of his extra-special exotic tins, it's very expensive, and we owe him some more money, an extra 2 pounds."

Grandma was fuming. She wouldn't be forgetting this in a hurry. But from across the room, Robin winked at Grandad, and Grandad nodded knowingly.

They both understood that the octopus trifle had saved the day, and made JP a very happy and popular little boy.